Rewind

Every man's memory is his private literature.
Aldous Huxley

Rewind

Edited by
Laura Thompson
Zara Little-Campbell
Kay Barnes

PARTHIAN

Parthian
The Old Surgery
Napier Street
Cardigan
SA43 1ED

www.parthianbooks.co.uk
www.rewindanthology.com

First published in 2008
© the authors 2008
All Rights Reserved

ISBN 978-1-905762-80-4

Editors: Laura Thompson
          Zara Little-Campbell
          Kay Barnes

Views expressed in these works are the authors'
own and do not necessarily reflect the opinions of
Trinity College or of Parthian.

Cover image by Marc Jennings
Cover design & typesetting by Lucy Llewellyn
Printed and bound by Dinefwr Press, Llandybïe, Wales

Published with the financial support of the Welsh
Books Council

British Library Cataloguing in Publication Data

A cataloguing record for this book is available from
the British Library

Rewind

Contents

Foreword

Was there ever a more contemporary image of our times than a remote control in the hand, the power to rewind this and that? It's a motif that's captured the imagination of a range of artists, from the severe last thoughts expressed in Severance by Robert Olen Butler, to the words of the song 'Rewind' by the Stereophonics:

If you could rewind your time
Would you change your life?

This year, the writers on the M.A. in Creative Writing programme chose a theme that would give them the freedom to roam into the past, through the mediums of fiction, drama and poetry. In so doing, they hoped to create new work that would also capture the 'zeitgeist' of our times.

This anthology therefore contains a great deal of hindsight, rewinding the past, while making language move forward, or, as Kiekegaard would have it, making sure that life is understood backwards even though it needs to be lived forward. I wonder if that is why emerging writers (and even long-established writers), still have the occasional difficulty with the present and past tense of verbs. How easy it is, in writing about the past, to still be locked within the present, or vice versa.

This year's contributors are as diverse as one could hope for, spanning seven decades between them. Is it any wonder therefore that we have such a rich fusion of language, from the heightened and poetic to the downright irreverent and gritty? The poetry within this collection ranges from poems akin to song lyrics, as presented by Kay Barnes, to a carefully-crafted sonnet of Llinos Jones. Zara Little Campbell's new take on Robert Frost reminds us that all writing is a palimpsest in one way or another; with her conversational style a stark contrast to the euphoric surrealism in 'Unseen images'. The sleight of hand poems of Enid Smith are cameos in which strangeness and familiarity blur with extreme lucidity.

Many of the stories in this anthology hanker back to a poignant past, as in the case of Jan Slade's delicate work. Likewise, a way of life dismantled in front of his eyes, brings forth almost a religious fervour in Alan Wakely's writings. A hilarious retelling of a romantic weekend at a hotel is entertainingly portrayed in Jo Perkins' story and Penny Sutton's vivid account of a reunion rekindles all kinds of vulnerabilities, and the way the past blightens our perspectives. Rob Morgan's meticulous, almost-Dosteyevskian, eye, conveys a shifting, moving landscape and an age where snow and weather has almost political overtones. Laura

Thompson's intriguing 'smoke long' stories manage to linger long in the mind.

This year the dramatists also presented us with memorable monologues. David Emrys Davies, Tyrone Deery and Tommy Maguire reflect a wry observation on life; between them they expose a derisive melancholia of life on the edge. These performance pieces, although meant for stage, display a grim humour; they also reveal the more unsavoury aspects of humankind. In a subtler tone and texture, Katy Griffiths's monologue slip-stitches faultlessly between outer and inner tensions.

So what are we to make of this collection? In the random access memory world of technology, it is reassuring that there are still experiences that resist easy codification. In this, the collective of writers have embarked on a journey that looks forward to new vistas but also looks back at the steps they have taken. Sometimes the 'echoes return slow' (as RS Thomas would have it). An attempt to freeze moments is as fitting as that of the frenetic images that the rewinding device brings forth. And could it be that the gadget, the rewinding device itself, is the 21st century's answer to the muse?

This year marks the eleventh year of the M.A. in Creative Writing at Trinity College, and once again it represents writers from Wales, England, Ireland and Canada. In a world where the dark side of globalism is always touched upon, here we have the uplifting light at its core. And what these writers hope for in their future is to achieve that 'forwarding' of their work, always moving forward as well as glancing back at what is left behind.

Menna Elfyn

My imagination runs colours
through the landscape that is my brain,
I think often of the past
but it's not always the same
Tommy Maguire

Consequences

Jan Slade

The operation had taken place the previous night and when she'd phoned from the call box at the end of the road they'd told her it had gone well.

'Come in tomorrow as usual,' they'd said, so there she was waiting for a bus on that cold, mid-March morning. She shivered in her thin, second-hand coat and prayed for the bus to hurry up; she'd a connection to make and if she missed it there would be another long wait for the next one.

At last her bus arrived and as she settled herself on the top deck she looked at her watch. Great, she had plenty of time. Her connection was at quarter to, and it was now just short of quarter past. Plenty of time for the twenty-minute journey and to spare.

She took the newspaper she had bought to while away the time and turned to the crossword. After five minutes or so she glanced out of the window and realised the bus had stopped

I

opposite a public house. She knew there was no bus stop nearby, and anyway it was too early for the pub to be open.

'What's going on?' she wondered, then saw the driver was coming out of the tall double gate in the wall. She watched as he stood at the edge of the pavement waiting to cross between the heavy traffic. Suddenly he glanced up and met her gaze. He grinned, shrugged his shoulders and mouthed 'Sorry', and she realised he'd used the pub's outside toilet. At last he managed to dodge his way through the cars and got into his cab.

The traffic was really building up now, she noticed as the bus edged its way from the kerb. Looking at her watch she was reassured to see that there was still plenty of time for her to catch her connection, and she went back to her crossword. The next thing she was aware of was the sound of an argument on the lower deck. Raising her head to listen she realised a man had tried to board without paying the fare and was resisting the driver's instruction to pay up or get off. After a lot of swearing and the threats of police being called, the passenger eventually left the bus, which continued on its way.

From then on every traffic light seemed to turn to red as the bus approached and she was beginning to get really uneasy about missing the connection. She put her newspaper away and, drumming her fingers nervously on the back of the seat in front, she leaned forward, anxiously watching the road ahead, and silently praying there would be no further delays. At last they reached the short road where the journey terminated. She rose and made her way to the stairs ready to jump off, but as they turned the corner she saw her connecting bus pull away.

'Oh, no, no!' she groaned aloud and almost fell down the

stairs as she slumped in frustration at the thought of the long hour's wait in front of her.

As she got off the bus she looked round for a telephone box. She wanted to phone the hospital to tell them she was delayed, and to find out how Claire was this morning. She'd had no time earlier, afraid of missing the bus, and now she wished she had taken the chance. With no call box in sight she went to the timetable display, desperately hoping she would find an alternative way of getting to the hospital, but there was none.

'What am I going to do?' she wailed inwardly. It was beginning to rain, her coat gave her little protection, and there was no shelter, not even a tree where she could hide from it. The weather added to her misery, and she began to pace up and down, tears joining the raindrops on her face. She looked in her purse, praying she would find enough money for a taxi, but she knew it was a forlorn hope; there was nothing for it but to wait.

By the time the bus arrived she was soaked through, shivering and blue with cold. She could hardly talk through her chattering teeth and the driver looked at her with concern as he handed her the ticket.

'You all right, love?' he asked, and she could only nod before sinking down into the nearest seat, trying to ignore the sympathetic glances of the other passengers.

They reached the hospital and she hurried into the building and up the stairs to the second floor.

Usually when she visited she donned one of the protective masks, which were placed in a dispenser outside the door of the small room where Claire was, and went straight in to see her baby. Eventually a nurse would find her there and they'd

3

discuss the baby's progress, but today she wanted to find out about the operation as soon as she could, so she went straight to the sister's office. Finding it empty she went into the main ward and saw the sister at the far end, talking to another nurse.

Smiling, she approached the women.

'I'm so sorry I'm late, I've had a dreadful journey. I missed my connection. How's Claire today? Is everything alright now?' The questions poured out in a babble of anxiety.

The sister hesitated before asking, 'Has anyone contacted you at home?'

The smile faded a little and she shook her head, puzzled.

'Contacted me at home? No, what do you mean?'

'Look, let's go to my office and I'll explain,' said the sister as she led the way.

Once settled in the small room the woman said, 'I'm sorry, but Claire took a turn for the worse this morning. We sent a police car to get you, and I thought they'd brought you here but obviously they missed you. I'm afraid, my dear, that Claire died twenty minutes ago.'

As the scream rose to her throat a little niggly thought came into her mind and in the days, months, years that followed it never went away.

If only...

The Hut

Zara Little-Campbell

Among the thick lime-green
Garden hedges, little hands
Found its weakness;
Opening a world concealed
From worrying adult eyes.

The leg-biting growth scrambled
To feel the flittering touch of
Sunlight; haphazard haven –
Each bramble mourned the loss
Of any member of its disfigured race.

Wild and remorseful playground –
It held many surprises: bits of buggies;
Grey-flecked bones; melted toys;
An assortment of literary treats
And the entrance to McGinley's
Derelict house.

The slim worn track meandered
Shamelessly through nature's
Greatest maze, in a small alcove

We claimed a space for our own;
Like cave men we hunted and gathered –
Mum's gold-rimmed cups and lemonade,
Dad's garden guides, upturned buckets
And pristine workman's tools –
We tamed the land and set up camp
One stolen bed-sheet at a time.

It became our time-capsule
A plea for existence – neatly smothered
In seasonal foliage and aging debris.
Around the campfire we sat,
The friend without a mother;
The boy without shoes;
And I, the girl without concerns;
We dissected the past of conflated
Memories and weaved a future in our
Dirty but enthusiastic palms.

Bunny

Laura Thompson

I tugged on his sleeve, pulling him toward the pet store. He kept his hands firmly in his pockets, and I ran ahead, pressing my nose against the window, staring at the animals on the other side like a puppy drooling over a fresh slipper.

A black and white puppy slept in the bottom right corner, curled up on a fuzzy white blanket. Kittens chased each other around in their small space, next to the sleeping puppy. Above them a small, beige bunny hopped toward me and pushed his nose against the window, against mine. I stroked the glass gently with one finger.

'Wait for me, Lexie.' Dad came up behind me and tentatively placed a hand on my shoulder, towering above me in our reflection in the window. 'Lexie, you don't want to look at those. Come on, we need to go find a present for Mum.'

'Yes, I do. Can we go in?'

'Lexie, we need to find a present for Mum.'

'Please,' I begged.

'Fine,' he said. 'But only for a minute.'

I ran into the store, and my dad reluctantly followed.

'Excuse me,' I said to the man wearing a pet store shirt. 'May I please hold the bunny in the window?'

'Sure, little lady.' I followed closely behind the man. He reached into the bunny's space and pulled out the pet I knew had to be mine. 'Here you are. Careful there.'

I cradled the bunny gently, showering it with tender kisses.

'Lexie, don't do that,' Dad said.

'I want one,' I answered softly, continuing to kiss the bunny.

'Lexie, you know we can't have one.'

'Are you sure?' He'd been saying this for ages, but maybe today I could change his mind. 'I'll watch him and clean up after him and play with him and—'

He cut me off with a sneeze. 'Lexie, I've told you over and over. We can't have a pet. End of story. Now give the bunny back to the man. I'll meet you outside.' He walked away, his eyes twitching with itch, his hands shoved back in his pockets.

I watched him for a moment then kissed the bunny one last time. 'One day, little lady,' the man said, taking my bunny away from me.

'Yeah.' I walked slowly out of the store and saw Dad waiting for me by a mall bench. Like kittens to catnip, I couldn't help but turn back. 'Bye, Bunny,' I said to my pet behind glass, and then followed my dad into the crowd of people in the mall, far away from the animals in the store. I hid my tears when we paid for the present for Mum. It was our only purchase of the day.

As we got into the car to leave the mall, I pouted. In the

back seat (I was too little to be allowed to sit in the front), I crossed my arms over my chest.

'Smile, Lexie,' Dad said, looking at me through the rearview mirror. 'Your mum will love the sweater we got her.'

'I bet she would have loved a bunny more.'

Dad looked away from me and started driving. We left the parking lot, the mall and the bunny. I stared out the window the whole way home and watched the houses whiz by. I wondered how many of those houses had bunnies inside them. Dad didn't say a word.

When we got home, I walked in the door behind my dad, still sulking.

'How was the shopping trip?' Mum asked.

'Good,' answered Dad.

I ran upstairs.

In my room I walked straight to my bookshelf. Instead of books, the top shelf was filled with bunnies. Plastic bunnies, porcelain bunnies, rubber bunnies, stuffed bunnies, piggy-bank bunnies. I had been collecting them since I could talk, since I could tell everyone that I wanted to start my own collection. Every year at my birthday and at Christmas, my collection grew. One year my parents gave me a stuffed bunny. I had many of those, but this one was my favourite. He got to sit at the front of the shelf. I liked him because he looked almost real. He was beige, about the size and shape of a baby bunny, and his whiskers tickled my cheeks. His dark brown eyes smiled at me. His fur was slightly worn and was stained from hopping around outside with me. I called him Bunny.

Dad walked into the room, and I ran to my bed. I got under my covers and pulled my thick, pale blue duvet all the way up to my chin. This was my refuge, an impenetrable fortress wall. Here I was safe and warm and could hide from the world.

Dad tried to pull the covers back a little, but I kept them wrapped tightly around me.

'Lexie, I'm sorry,' he said. 'I wish we could have a rabbit, but we really can't.'

'You're not sorry. You don't understand. I want one so much. I've wanted one my whole life, and you won't let me have one.'

'Lexie, you saw me sneeze. I can't be doing that all the time.'

'I know,' I sighed. 'I just really wish I could have one. I can't help it. I'm in love.'

He smiled sympathetically. 'I know. I really am sorry.' He leaned forward and kissed me on the forehead, stroking my hair at the same time. I looked up at him in surprise. I wasn't used to my dad kissing me. 'Supper's ready.' He pulled away quickly and walked downstairs, leaving me to my duvet fort.

I let it collapse and sat up in bed, watching my dad leave.

The next morning I woke up to see Dad sitting on my bed again. I kept the duvet pulled tight against my chin. 'Lexie, I have something for you,' he said.

'You do? But it's Mum's birthday, not mine.'

'I know.'

'What is it?' I asked, starting to get excited.

Dad picked something up from beside the bed: a home-made bunny cage. The four sides of a box had been cut out, leaving only a cardboard frame. Replacing those sides was chicken wire. What was left of the cardboard had been painted pale blue, and there was a latch on one end where I noticed a flap for a door. Sitting inside was my stuffed Bunny.

'I really wish I could give you a real bunny. I'm sorry that I can't, but I hope this helps.'

I smiled, came out from under my covers, and gave my dad a huge hug. He squeezed me back, stroking my hair and giving me another peck on the forehead. 'Now, come on,' he said. 'Let's go back to the mall and get that bunny some bunny toys.'

'Okay!' I said, jumping out of bed. Dad went downstairs, leaving me to get ready. I quickly put my clothes on. Then I picked up the cage, opened its cardboard door, and petted Bunny as gently as I would a real rabbit.

At the mall, I ran to the pet store again, and my dad kept up with me. Proudly, I walked straight into the store without looking at the puppy and the kittens, and stealing only one small glance at the beige bunny in the window. Inside, I found a miniature blanket that would fit nicely inside my new bunny cage. I picked a bag of fake straw to make a comfy bed for my new pet. I even found a toy carrot for Bunny to chew. Dad paid for my choices, and I told the man at the cash that they were for my new bunny. 'One day,' he had said yesterday. 'Today's the day,' he said now, grinning at me. I nodded, returning only half a grin and looking intently at the scuffed wooden floor.

Dad put one hand in his pocket, took my hand with his other one, and we walked out of the store together. As we passed by the front window, I made sure he wasn't looking, then snuck a look at the real bunny. It hopped to the window and pressed its nose against the glass. Dad and I walked away, and I clutched the new little blanket tightly against my chest.

The School Reunion

Penny Sutton

'We're going to my old school reunion on our next home visit.'

'Oh yes,' not really thinking too much about it at the time. The oracle had spoken and would be obeyed.

Two very different people, brought up in different countries on different continents; our home now is miles from either. We compare school days: an all girls' boarding school in South Africa and a co-educational grammar school, purporting to be at the leading edge of British education in the 1950s. It was hard for me to imagine it, especially as, at the time, I would have been stumbling around in nappies.

So this means another merry-go-round of visiting relations. How many nights do I have to build up for this time? I didn't meet his parents before we married, and somehow visits put a tremendous strain on us both. He's an only child, doted on, can never do any wrong! He and his mother fight like caged ferrets, they're so alike. I feel like a nightclub bouncer trying to placate rowdy revellers; father-in-law looks on smiling, 'they've always been like this'.

So I find myself being driven around the Leicestershire countryside on a slightly overcast summer Saturday. Hanging baskets adorn the roadside pubs; their brilliant pinks, reds, purples and yellows thrust themselves into my line of vision, splashing colour against white painted walls. 'And this is where we used to go fishing,' he reminisces, pointing to a quaint wooden bridge over the river Soar. And 'that used to be a swimming pool, there was an outcry when it was pulled down, and celebrations when the huge public library opened.'

'Oh yes,' I answer, trying to find enthusiasm when I am really dreading this afternoon's visit.

It's all new and, for someone brought up in a one-street town in the middle of nowhere, very confusing but interesting to see. I can't think why it is that Mike so loves the middle of Africa, compared with this green and pleasant land.

'Where did you live then?' I ask timidly.

'Oh, we'll visit that on the way back, it's way over the other side of town, make us horribly late.'

That would be fine by me as I proffer, 'Oh, OK.'

The car park at the old school has a line of cars, mostly new – an MGB GT in bright racing green, a silver Jaguar E Type and a bright red Ford Capri all boasting the latest number plates. Our borrowed Mini Clubman looks very much like the poor relation. Mike parks it beside the newest car he can find, enjoying bucking the obvious one-upmanship display.

The building is fabulous, weathered old red brick with ornate external lintels and turrets at each end of it; high windows – so that bored teenagers can't be distracted, I suspect! Playing fields stretch almost as far as the eye can see, muddied goal mouths litter the grassed area, a rich array of old established oak, ash and sycamore trees make their distinctive silhouettes on the skyline, framing an early harvest of hay bales scattered on the fields beyond.

We're greeted in a huge porchway with cracking Victorian tiles; I imagine hordes of spotty-faced youngsters sheltering out of the weather as they wait to go into school. Solid wooden floors, scuffed from hundreds of muddy shoes with laces dangling behind them, still give off the slightest smell of old wood. Ancient desks, with 'R loves J, xxx' carved on the old-fashioned hinged lid, are pushed up against the side walls, giving plenty of space for people to mingle. Mike runs his hand along the surface of one desk, lifts the lid; inside is ink stained, pockets of fluff and detritus from schoolboys', and possibly schoolgirls', pockets collect in the corners. He closes it and mimes 'memories' to me.

'Hi Gina, what are you up to now?' And then almost as an afterthought, 'Oh you haven't met my wife.' I smile shyly in the background, offering a limp hand, as she regales him with her recent promotion to consultant gynaecologist at the city's teaching hospital.

'I thought you were going into law?'

'No, that's Morag, she's now a barrister, covers mostly south of here – very well thought of by all accounts, she's always too busy to meet up.'

'Oh, and there's Faye, must go and tease her, she always wanted help with her maths, nice little earner that was for me! Don't think they ever found out.'

'She's a headteacher now, somewhere in Cornwall.'

'She'll be well placed, knowing what the youth of yesterday got up to!'

'Keep a look out for Keith, said he was coming.'

'And Tim. Is he here?'

'Yes, but only for a short while, has to get back to the children, it's his turn to have them this weekend. You must catch up with him.'

Children, I think to myself, of course they're all fifteen years older than me, their kids'll be on the waiting list to come here. We can't afford them, not at the moment, hardly got a penny to our names, and both working frantically to put some cash together. My pittance lasts us a week! And then we struggle with his. But we're happy, aren't we? Well I am, aren't I? Not so sure at this precise moment; I think I want to be back in the sub Saharan sun.

I turn to look at Mike; he's not that good looking, tall with a mop of black curly hair framing his tanned face. His olive skin against mine makes him look almost Mediterranean. But he's honest-to-God English, as his father always reminds me. I presume he thinks my ancestry is dubious; he's never met anyone born outside of the country.

A small woman, impeccably dressed, sidles up to me: 'Oh, you must be Rachael?' Her tailored straight navy skirt cuddles the smallest hips I have ever seen; the hemline, just above the knee, shows her delicately shaped legs below. A neat box-shaped cream jacket with navy piping around the lapels shows off an expensive looking pale blue silk blouse beneath.

'Er, yes,' I stutter, looking round frantically for Mike. At his height he's easy to spot, but he's nowhere to be seen. She must have sensed my uneasiness and seemed to be enjoying my humiliation. I keep my eyes roaming the room willing Mike to appear and release me from this ordeal.

'Come and get a cup of tea.' Did I sense a hint of sarcasm

in the voice? 'I'm sure he's around here somewhere.'

'Oh, thanks,' I reply meekly, trying not to appear terrified.

'When did you get here, to England I mean?'

'On Thursday.' Why isn't Mike here to answer these questions?

'How long are you staying?'

'Three weeks, all the leave we've got.'

'At least the weather is being kind for you.'

'Yes,' I reply timidly, still unaware who I'm speaking to.

'Oh Paul, have you seen Mike? Come and meet his wife.' She seems to be revelling in my isolation. I can feel my face colouring, embarrassing beads of perspiration trickle off my forehead; I turn my head quickly, hoping to displace them.

I'm slowly being surrounded by people, people I don't know, in a strange place. They all seem very friendly. Why do I feel so out of my depth? Their designer attire makes me conspicuous in my homemade clothes. We can't buy anything ready made at home, and currency restrictions limit our overseas expenditure. I tug at my mini skirt, willing it to lengthen! Was it last year's fashion here? They all look at me, is it genuine concern or pity? I smile, hope he will come and save me from my ordeal.

'Could we all move into the Geography Room folks, Dr Hawker is going to give us a talk,' a middle-aged man addresses the room.

I follow the group, anxious. Where's he got to?

'Hi, you OK?'

'Where've you been?' I hiss.

'Oh just revisiting a few old haunts.'

'Thanks. Please don't just leave me.'

They all talk among themselves, barracking Dr Hawker;

he's obviously one of the old timers. We would never have spoken to our teaching staff like that. Can't imagine a school reunion of mine, folk have all moved away, all over the world.

I try to remember names Mike has mentioned in our conversations of old. Who did what? So many names it's impossible to link anything together.

'Well folks, I won't keep you from the bar any longer. Good to see you all, have a drink on the old school.'

Choruses of cheers ring round the room; the blokes gather together around the bar, like pins swarming onto a magnet. The girls move off too, to the ladies I assume; I follow and hope, for what I'm not sure.

'You OK?'

'Yes fine. Is the loo this way?'

'Follow us.' They march off chattering, ignoring me.

Is Gina about? She seemed friendly. Ah there's the ladies, I pop in.

The noise takes me back to the blokes. They're getting rowdier, glasses chinking.

'Remember the bike sheds?' someone laughs, 'They've knocked them down, how dare they!'

'Yeh, maybe they don't need to hide their fags these days? P'raps its drugs today. At least in our day it was just a good old pint.'

'Or two, or three,' comes from the fringes.

I wander off to look at books, left open for inspection. These must be photos of them all. I look closely, is he there?

'There you are. Having a nice time?'

'Yes,' I lie. 'These are interesting.'

'That was when we all played rugby for the county schools team. That's me, Paul on the left and Dave, can't recognise the other arses. They all look the same covered in mud and cowshit. Did you get a drink?'

'No, is there a Coke?'

I'm twisting the end of my belt. They're all in their own groups, anyone would think I'm invisible. I think I'm the only spouse.

'There you go.' A Coke is plonked in my hand. 'Oh, I must just go and catch up with Ricky. You'll be OK, won't you?'

I suppose I will, 'Yes, sure.'

I go back to look through the exhibitions, I don't know what to say to anyone. The chaps are all well oiled, the girls seem to be in a corner, like a WI meeting. I wish I wasn't here. I want to go, go anywhere, even back to the in-laws would be preferable to this.

He must have sensed my anguish, 'You ready then?'

'Yes.'

'You'd better drive.'

'You'll have to give me directions, I don't know where I am.'

'Yes, sure.'

I weave our little Mini between the row of expensive cars; I've not long had a licence, driving here is such an effort, loads of traffic, twists and turns, road signs at every junction, all very confusing.

'Which way now?'

Silence from the passenger seat, the gentle snoring of a well inebriated passenger hums round the car. I follow the signs for 'City Centre,' almost sure we go towards it to take the ring road.

'Hey, Mike, which way do I go? Please wake up.'

'Yes, that's right.' And he promptly closes his eyes, deeper snores reverberate around the car. We do get home, eventually. I dread to think what would have happened had I not stumbled on a familiar road. I go cold at the thought. I leave him to negotiate with his fellow ferret while I go upstairs and change into something warmer.

'Never again,' I say to the mirror, 'not for anything,' trying to fight back the tears.

*****

'Remember the Reunion? It must be nearly twenty years ago.'

'Oh Mike, how can I ever forget? Total humiliation, God I've never known such a gathering of the great and the good. And me, a mere typist, just eighteen.'

'Oh I don't know...'

'I do, a total disaster!'

'But you survived.'

'Only just, not helped by you either.'

'What d'you mean?'

'I've never seen you quite so drunk, I hadn't a clue where I was going. No sat nav in those days.'

'Yeh, but you got me home.'

'That's not the point. Never again...'

'No, me too. But...'

'But what?'

'I suppose I should have mentioned this before...'

'Hmmm...'

'Remember Gina mentioned Tim?'

'Yeh.'

'Well I went off to find him. I had a score to settle.'

Mike was wriggling, what was coming I needed to know and now. 'Go on.'

'Well, by the time I had done the rounds he had disappeared. I came back to find you and you were in conversation with Sue.'

'Which one was that? There were so many new faces.'

'The little one, dressed in blue I think.'

'Oh, her. She seemed to know an awful lot about me and I couldn't work out why.'

'Ah well.

'Spit it out.'

'We were, well they would say "an item" today.'

I sat back and listened, intrigued; no wonder she was so curious about me. I felt spooky, I had gate-crashed his former life; no wonder it was such an ordeal.

'Well then Tim got his oar in and it was all Tim and Sue this and Tim and Sue that. I felt utterly betrayed. I tried so hard to win her back, but she wasn't having it. And, yes, she and Tim got married. That's when I went abroad, couldn't stand the atmosphere.'

'So...'

'Hang on, I haven't finished. She always kept in touch, just to remind me of my loss I suppose. The bitch. I used to rip up her letters when they arrived. It was hard enough getting over her without having to be reminded constantly.'

'But you knew she was coming?'

'No, Paul said Tim would be there. That's why I wanted to go.'

'Why draw me into all this then?'

'I needed you there, I needed your support.'

'Oh yeh, you hardly saw me all afternoon.'

'No, I couldn't face seeing her again or so I thought and then I opened her last letter and read it. She was having problems with Tim and she wanted to see me. Of course I never replied, I didn't want to be used. It was then Paul told me Tim would be there and it was obvious she wouldn't.'

'Where is all this leading? She was there.'

'I know, she must have found out from somebody. One of the girls I assume. But she collared me later in the afternoon and propositioned me.'

'I didn't notice that.'

'No you wouldn't, she made quite sure you were out of the way. Well I can't say it didn't resurrect the old feelings I had for her.'

'Now you tell me.'

'Hey, Rach hang on, let me finish. I then tried to get to you, realising that it might help the problem, but she was so insistent and started raising her voice and I didn't want you suspecting anything. Well... that was when I hit the bar, I offered to get her a drink and just stayed with the chaps. Felt it was safer that way.'

'Oh.' What else was there to say? It was beginning to explain things.

'That's not all. The next I get a phone call from Tim accusing me of trying to get off with her at the school reunion. Rich coming from him! He goes on to tell me they have split up but he is trying to get things back together again, he was coming for an hour or so and would then look after the kids so she could catch up with her pals. Gives me an earful, accuses me of luring her away. I laughed.'

'But you...'

'I know, I did make some suggestive comments, but you know me – I only half meant them!'

'Yeh, which half?'

'Surely that's fairly obvious now? And anyway look what the day did for you?'

'A real live lecture on self help in humiliation you mean?'

'No, dafty. Ever thought what you have achieved compared with that motley crew? I think it is them who would be intimidated by you now.'

'Yeh, yeh, yeh. Compliments, to dig yourself out of a hole.'

'Hey, that's not fair. I now know who I would prefer to be with.'

'Heard from Tim lately?'

'No, just wish him luck with the old bat, if they got back together again.'

Unseen Images

Tommy Maguire

I've seen German Paratroopers converge on the Somme to dance by the moonlight,
Their dresses catch the silver streaks of shimmer endlessly.
I've seen a rhapsody being played by a two-month-old hen,
Before a shrew devoured the sheet music.
I've seen infinite flamingos biting their nails in frustration,
Never ready for the attack on their feet.
I've seen a man on the tube talk to his own hair,
Ignoring the ticket inspector arguing with his shoes.
I've seen a Sioux Chef pray to a square pea,
Before a lobster boiled him alive.
I've seen a groom fuck his wedding cake,
Whilst his wife cried with pride.
I've seen an egg scramble itself in respect to fallen comrades,
The sausage empire is still ruling impassively.
I've seen televisions watch people,
They cry when they're turned off.
I've seen piglets suckling the teats of a Panda,
They devoured the wretched bitch from the inside out.
I've seen the Americas crumble,
It made me feel all tingly inside.
I've seen the end of this sentence,
This is how I remember it.

Back to the Truth

Katy Griffiths

Kara sat at her dressing table, staring at her reflection in the mirror, willing her face to change, willing the shape to change; to become somebody else, something else; anybody different from the person that she was now; the person that she had become. According to *him* anyway. He who knew everything. He who was never, ever wrong.

You just can't let it go, can you? You can't waste any opportunity to remind me, to rub it in. Do you think I don't remember? Do you think I've forgotten? Stuck in the past, that's what you are; all bitter and twisted and self righteous to boot.

Bitter and twisted; she imagined a photograph thrown onto the fire, curling up, crumpling into itself, as if to escape the charred blackness of the edges as the fire slowly ate into it, destroying the centre and then engulfing it whole. Was that really the person she had become? The words flashed through

27

her like a knife, like a sword; words that sliced her open and forced her to see what was really inside. She *had been* bitter; who wouldn't be bitter after everything she'd gone through? But that was over now. Or at least she thought it was. It was starting to bubble of late; starting to bubble and boil, and simmer on the surface. Ever since that phone call last night.

She continued to stare at her face in the mirror, willing her features to morph back to the way they used to be when she was a teenager, when she met him for the first time. She looked so different then, before worry lines started to creep across her forehead, before bags began to drop under her eyes. She never thought herself very pretty, not like her sisters, not like Millie, not like Abbie, not like Olivia.... She flinched, jerking her head away, as if to stop those thoughts from entering her head; she doesn't think about those times much. She didn't. Until now.

It's not as if I don't have good reason to feel this way. You'd feel like this if I'd done that to you. Maybe I'll go out tonight, forget about you for a few hours, like you forgot about me. The door slammed behind her, him making his usual exit; her shuddering slightly, shaking clever retorts out of her head. This didn't happen that often; normally they co-existed quite comfortably; the past floating easily underneath their feet without needing to be dredged up and raked over; she trying desperately to keep the mental image of him and... *her* wedged firmly at the back of her mind. But not any more, she couldn't hold it back; ever since Abbie phoned it had been right at the front of her forehead.

'Hi babe, it's Abbie. Listen, I know this is difficult but you have to come back. Mum is asking for you, she needs to see you. The doctors said she might not have much.... You can't stay away just because Olivia might be here. You two have to get over this. Please Kara. You need to move on.'

Move on. Just like that, move on. She'd done that already, she'd moved on, moved away and yet still it followed her, dragged behind her, limp and disjointed like a broken limb. But maybe you had to go back before you could move on, exorcise a few ghosts, lay a few demons to rest and drop off some emotional baggage on your way. She would go back, for Abbie's sake. Abbie, who had always tried to stay neutral, not to take sides, even though she knew what Olivia had done was wrong. *But how do you know that she did it? I know it because I saw her. Admittedly from the back, from a distance, but that was enough.* She'd denied it, of course she had. What else could she do? But Kara knew; she'd seen her looking at him and she knew.

And now she would see her again. And now she would admit the truth.

Abbie stared languidly out of the small slatted windows, gazing out at the grassy land ahead, quiet and still, beyond the trees. Too quiet really. Even at this hour of the day, there was always something going on, some movement, some murmur; a buzz or hum floating across from some distant landscape, which caught and snagged on the corners of the white-washed house. But no, nothing today, not a whisper; not even a hint. But then this place had changed, she had changed; it had been years since she'd slept within these walls.

She shifted her position slightly, pain shooting up her back as the wooden chair beneath her refused to yield, the legs creaking, as if somehow sympathetic to her suffering. She glanced around anxiously. Nobody moved, nobody stirred, nobody inched out of the positions they had been holding for hours now. They just sat there, waiting, watching, still, whilst silence echoed through the room, bouncing off the walls and whirling around the bed where her mother lay, still and empty, surrounded by a dull grey hue. She hadn't said anything for hours now. It would surely be over soon.

She rested her head against the chair back and tried once again to get some sleep. Sleep had been proving fairly elusive of late, turning on its heel and refusing to return her calls, no matter how many sheep she counted; so many things weighing on her mind and dragging it down like a boulder. Olivia would be here soon; they would all be together, in the same room for the first time in years, and then there would be trouble. It would be like lighting the touch paper, standing back, waiting for the fireworks to ignite, and hoping others don't get burnt in the process. She tried to tell herself it would be easier now, years had gone by, people had changed. It was all in the past, though she remembered it well, as if it were yesterday, in spite of her many attempts to forget. She wasn't involved in the arguments and explosions that were a daily occurrence around the house, trying to stay out of them as far as she could, mainly because she had other things on her mind. It wasn't long after that she discovered she was pregnant, yet another shame to be inflicted on her mother. Still, her crime seemed miniscule by comparison, and at least she wouldn't be a single parent, Daniel having proved himself very committed in the past. That was the one thing she was sure about; that he would stand by her, look after her, no matter what, so she never felt that she had made the wrong decision, marrying him. He was a good father to Luke, a good choice. She had told herself that so many times over the years, lying in bed, staring at the ceiling cracks and counting the cost. Everyone made mistakes.

She sat up, rubbing her neck to ease the silent protest it had been inflicting upon her, and let out a long breath through pursed lips, pushing through the air like a blade slicing, disturbing the dust settled in the congealed atmosphere. *Once the dust has settled.* She had heard that so many times in this house as well. *She'll get through it; it'll all blow over soon enough.* It didn't quite happen that way though, as getting through it took time and nobody had that much time, without their patience snapping and twanging like an elastic band. To Abbie's mind, seeing Kara and Chris perched there on wooden chairs, poker straight and conspicuously separate, things had already blown over, like a tree snapped off in the winds. The damage was already done.

The doorbell rang, jolting her out of her solitude; the sharp clanging chime chewing its way through the house. The effect was immediate, as if an electric current had passed through the air and everybody, Kara, Chris, Daniel, Luke and Millie, all sat up, alert and intensified. The dust would have to settle all over again because outside the door, trouble was coming, ringing the doorbell and demanding to be heard.

Olivia stood nervously at the doorway; finger poised above the doorbell, as if she couldn't quite believe that she had just pressed it. She glanced around at the yard surrounding her; a path that she had navigated many times before, though in those days, it had felt like a minefield, with unknown bombs and snipers, and Olivia had been in the firing line more than most. It still hurt to think how easily her mother had sided with Kara, the sting not entirely gone from its tail. She hadn't even waited to hear Olivia's side of things, probably assuming that there wasn't a side to be heard, that there was no possible defence she could make, other than complete denial, which was the only defence she had. She shivered slightly, memories of long ago arguments bristling down her backbone. She tried to forget, she tried to pretend, but it was no good. The scar was still visible, still red, still raw.

She was surprised by how changed it was, how dilapidated, how shabby, with peeled-off layers of paint exposing the bare fading flesh, in various shades of lifeless. She always remembered this place in colours, but that was all gone now; everything seemed drained away, as if someone had pulled a plug, leaving only brown residue, scum on the surface, second-hand dirt. Bit like her, in a way. At least that's what they all said about her. Whether it was true or not didn't seem to matter.

Footsteps crackled through the house, barking briskly along the slabs and whispering along the carpet. Daniel pulled back the door and smiled at her. Welcoming; so different from the others, he never bore grudges, never clung onto the past like barnacles to a rock. He hadn't changed much, but then he'd always looked young, even when he was young, so he was always out of time's reach somewhat. The last time they met was at the wedding, to which she was grudgingly invited by her mother, at Abbie's request. No, invited wasn't the right word; permitted seemed more accurate, as if she didn't have any real right to be there at all. It had all ended in tears of course; Kara had made a scene; Kara who could never keep her mouth shut; Kara who could never resist inflicting her misery upon others. Mother must have been so proud that day, standing at the church in her big hat, new frock and corsage bedecked handbag, proof that at least one of her children was capable of obtaining a husband that didn't belong to someone else, preferably her sister. Nobody spoke to her, much less stood next to her, leper that she was rapidly becoming. But Daniel was never like that. Maybe that was why Abbie liked him. He had a solid, sturdy, dependable feel to him, like an old oak tree well rooted in the ground, although physically that couldn't be further from the truth. Very different from Chris, whose body was his currency; his temple that he strutted about trying to find worshippers for; a man who probably spent more time on his hair than a collection of women in toilets. All of which made it surprising that he went out with Kara, who was prim, proper and precise; the female equivalent of a buttoned-up beige cardigan, inviting the vicar to tea. Even more surprising that he'd married her, as Chris regarded a wife as a trophy, a medal, and only a gold one would do. They would be here, of course, as Kara was never able to resist running to Mummy, and she couldn't have left him at home. She didn't have a long enough leash. She'd make a scene, naturally, raking up the past that was once so fully dead and buried. Olivia knew this would happen; she was expecting it, she was dreading it, but she came anyway. She just wanted one last try, one last look before the door finally closed and everything was settled.

Slowly, cautiously, she stepped inside. Her shoe heel clacked sharply on the flags.

'You've got some nerve showing your face here. Why the hell did you bother coming? You've got no right...'

'Excuse me, I have every right, she's my mother.'

'You gave up that right a long time ago, when you ran away, tail between your legs. Who are you to come swanning back?'

'And who are you to say I can't?'

Millie sat gingerly on the chair, not moving, not stirring, not even breathing. She was too afraid to say anything in case they both turned on her, anger capable of swivelling and changing in an instant. She had seen this too many times. It was just like this all those years ago, when she was a child, hovering on the stairs, silent witness to the downstairs destruction. Nobody told her anything, older sisters having a fondness for keeping their business to themselves, but she found a way. Nobody would notice her anyway. She had got quite accomplished at not being noticed.

'There's no place for you here, you do realise that, don't you? Nobody wants you here.'

It was so strange, these arguments. When she was young she didn't really understand; not that she had much idea now. It didn't make any sense.

'No, it's only you who doesn't want me here.'

She could never understand why Kara was so angry at Olivia all the time. She just couldn't work it out.

'And surely you can see why I don't want you here, you cheating...'

'I've told you before, it wasn't me. I never did anything with your husband.'

'Well, if it wasn't you, who was it? Go on, tell me, who was it?'

She couldn't understand why Chris had married Kara when really he liked Abbie. She'd seen them together, one day, years and years ago, not that long before all the arguments started. She remembered it well, though she was only young. Small and agile, she was adept at creeping into places where she couldn't be seen, where she couldn't be noticed.

'I don't know who it was. How do you expect me to know that? You just don't listen, you get one idea stuck in your head and that's it. You don't even give anyone else a chance.'

Olivia stormed out, slamming the door behind her, a dull echo running resonant throughout the house. Millie stared around the room; everybody else was silent, unmoving, still. She glanced over at Kara, staring intently out of the window at Chris entertaining Luke, both having escaped at the first sound of gunfire. She wondered if Kara was thinking the same thing that she was, if she too was noticing how much alike they were and how they seemed to smile at the same things and how their blue eyes both seemed to twinkle mischievously in the exact same way.

The Girl at the Bus Stop

Enid Smith

A bottle blonde, long tendrils straight and sharply
Cut to the fashion, hanging round her face.
Her eyes are blue, a lovely sapphire hue
With lashes, thick and heavy, black with kohl
So, when she raises eyes to see, they droop
And give a lang'rous look, a slanting swoop
Fluttering on her silken cheek, beneath brows
Which loop, festooned with chains and golden beads.
Her nostrils gently flare and from each ear
Is shackled, linked to lobes and lips
So full, and ripe it ill behoves to sip
Or even smile, for since her tongue is split
With globes of glist and gold
So, when she talks or eats, she spits.

We haven't finished with this maid's attire
She's not bereft of suitors set afire.
Her suit is black in classic cut and long
The jacket, while the trews sling low, below
Her lightly tanned and rounded belly
Sports rings above a silver Spanish belt
And on her feet, flamenco boots, black leather calf

So when she walks, she strides out well
Men young and old admire and they can tell
This girl's a mind to challenge, not repel
Not one to emulate in any way,
                    but every girl must have her day
Afraid of no one, who could wish her harm?

A Chapel in Blaina

Alan Wakely

It is the afternoon of yesterday. One of many winter yesterdays and it is neutral. It is neither warm, nor possessed of winter's vicious nip. The sun has given some comfort, except in the fearing corners that live in shadow.

I stood outside the library checking my pockets for keys and wallet and specs; across the road, perched on a grass carpeted mound as verdant as in summer, but surrounded by trees as bare as bones in a grave, it stands.

It could be Salem, Bethlehem, Soar or Berea, but it is not. It has in the past acknowledged the same Trinity, but now, roofed only by the sky, both man and God can see its heart. There is no wind in its lungs to lift praise to the rafters; there are no chords, bellowed, pumped and keyed to resonate among its varied stones. Long gone, the Sunday fresh face, clearing its throat and conscience, gargling for redemption and dying for a pee. No more the Minister, reconciled to volume, muttering: 'Sing you buggers, sing,' and grateful for his deaf ear. There are no coins, warm from the pocket and cold from the purse, telling tales of parsimony syllable by chinking syllable to a commodious salver.

This place has outlived its purpose, it has no function and thus, it is redundant. For a few short-lit weeks it will continue to offer fragile testimony as it disintegrates. And somewhere, briefly, a memory will recall the day the last stone fell, when the last leaf left the trees, and the last voice, cracked with age, deceived by Dementia, croaked the last hymn.

This unremarkable chapel is being razed by less fearful hands than those that built it. And there is no remorse or fear of retribution, and no lament. God is no longer wanted, God is in retreat.

At the doorway I looked in. Not a pew remained, their seasoned, scented pine lay outside, riven from the floor and wrenched from the New Testament with indiscriminate disregard. The floors, thrown to the flames, split and splintered, burned to the crack of sparks and clouded heaven to the tear.

The windows, high arched, open to the elements, their coloured Saints shattered and beyond appeal peck at the soles of Philistines. The pulpit stands, just, incapable of supporting a page, let alone a complete Bible; it is mute and unable to amplify a priest's purging percussion.

There are four men working, black to the brow, plugged in to music from mobile phones and over-drummed by the thud of a Honda generator that powers a machine cutting to its own

scream. There are eight ornate cast iron columns supporting
the skeletal remains of the upper floor; they are plain and
fussy in design, self-consciously Victorian, hopeful for belief
in their cold piety. The organ oversees the destruction.

Silent.   Resigned.

Not a whisper through its asthmatic reeds, ivories and pedals
have gone to scrap; and a man is whistling as he tears the
pipes out; he is a vulture at a carcass. The hymns are gone,
and the last sermon from Tudor ap Dafydd, a man thinner
than a match with the wood shaved off, was lost to the echo
among the incontinent, impatient for his final, tubercular
words to fall from his blood-dead lips.

In this unpriested place, lost to its Easters, Whitsuns and
Christmas pleadings, I feel I must have something, not out of
sadness, I did not know it when it was alive, and not in
deference to the God to whom I entrust my unqualified soul,
and not for any pecuniary value I may turn to advantage, no,
I am dispassionately curious.

I ask for a pipe from the organ.

A small one... because... I want to hold something I have
never been this close to, and the nearer, perhaps, my God, to
Thee?

The Clockmaker

Rob Morgan

The ancient bus coughed to a halt on the edge of the square. Without delay a swarm of shabby passengers, mostly women, a handful of old men and children, spewed forth onto the cobbles, and slipped away among the stalls of the market. They were late, and their lateness lent them urgency.

Market day was ending. Snow was banged from ragged tarpaulins that still bore the emblem of the Reich, or even of the old Republic. Cataracts of vegetables rumbled like muddy cannonballs onto the bottom of rough carts, and two or three lean horses were being backed with foul oaths and useless gestures between the shafts.

Ruddy-cheeked farmers and their wives, better fed than the townsfolk, gathered around the braziers and glanced apprehensively at the swiftly changing sky as they stamped their straw-stuffed boots, gnawed hard black bread, munched onions and jingled coins in grumbling pockets.

He was the last to leave the bus. The second his feet touched the cobbles the driver eased the struggling engine into life and the bus rattled away down a narrow side street. For a moment he looked about the familiar place, pulling the old military greatcoat close about him for what little warmth it could provide. The last fight of the dying Wehrmacht had cost the little medieval town dear; missing houses left gaps like rotten, vanished teeth, faded slogans stained walls, and scars from bombardment left gashes across roof and gable. There were few men in the square, so few men anywhere now. Sitting silently on the jolting bus journey from the far-off station he had listened to women discussing as women had since the war ended, how soon the prisoners in the east would return.

Six years. He smiled wryly. He knew that prison cold, and that long darkness. Maybe one in twenty would come back. Six years? Maybe one in fifty.

If they ever did.

His ears quickly became accustomed to the dark dialect shouted across the flurry of poultry and the squeal of pigs goaded from half-dismantled pens as farmers eager to depart before the snow returned stacked the hurdles; disregarding the few townsfolk who lingered in their way, exchanging familiar greetings with each other.

Was it really almost Christmas?

A rich metallic sound struck the frozen air. The man looked upwards at the clock tower. Apart from a long scar where a streak of shrapnel had unlaced its face, the clock stood intact. Just as it had for four centuries, through war after war, and season after season. He slipped his hand into his greatcoat pocket, touching the leather cloth that covered the pistol.

Half past three o'clock.

The momentary silence which had taken the square by surprise passed, and the flurry of human activity continued, as rapidly as the light began to fade from the old town. His one brief glance at the clock was enough, the rest he could recall from his boyhood. The enormous town hall roof, tiled with the scales of dragons his grandfather had told him; shields carved in high-relief with double-headed Imperial eagles leaned out from the walls of the high gilded tower.

The man turned away, slipping out of the square across the slush of last night's snowfall, on army boots that probably wouldn't outlast the winter.

No one noticed him.

Just another former soldier going nowhere, another solitary soul looking for nothing in particular. Unremarkable, unkempt, unfamiliar even in the place where he was born.

A flight of elegant, ruined steps led to the lower part of the town. Here the upper storeys almost touched across the lanes. A warren of carpenters and saddlers and smithies and cave-like workshops threw light into the already darkening narrow way between them. A rushing workman brushed hard against him, and his hand swiftly moved to his pistol to protect it from discovery.

He liked the gun. A Polish Pistolet Radom wzor 35, heavy, it weighed over a kilogram, but a faultless weapon. At close range the eight 9mm rounds would destroy anything that breathed and did not run. The last one, the toymaker, had run but only as far as the stairs of his workshop; erupting his last breath as he clutched for the little Langenham automatic protruding from his jacket. How appropriate, the man had thought as he stepped over the ruptured corpse, a toy pistol for a toymaker. Hell, those things were around in the old Kaiser's day.

A second heavy clang sounded. The clock struck again, a hundred metres behind him.

A quarter to four.

Soon. The fellow would move soon. He passed the clockmaker's shop, barely glancing in through the forest of swaying pendulums and stuttering hands into the lamplight, to where the craftsman sat over the debris of a vast device. It looked every bit as complex as that which had killed his soldiers that last, frozen night of panic and flight.

The new arrival stepped off the icy cobbles where the wind blew hard and cold down the hill, into a small tavern close by. He stood silently at the low window, throwing back his schnapps as he saw the clockmaker trim his lamp, pull on his coat, and lock his workshop door. Every Friday Market Day the clockmaker climbed the tower steps, as generations of his predecessors had for four hundred years, and as soon as the clock had struck four he rewound the fine renaissance mechanism, and admired as his forebears would the beauty of the enduring changeless machinery.

The clockmaker looked to neither right nor left as he climbed the steep steps to the town square for the last time. The square was empty now, as darkness fell quickly, the last few carts departing to the echo of shouted farewells, and the sounds of distant animals.

Snow was beginning to fall again.

It would be a cold night for those who lived through it.

A few dim lights showed into the open square, some small noise from a corner drinking-house; a late villager swathed in sacks leading a vast horse drifted into shadow and was gone.

The man stood in darkness next to a heavy pillar scarred by rifle fire. As the clockmaker wielded the huge key to the tower door, he stepped silently forwards. Bent almost double from decades of ticking and tinkering, the craftsman softly closed the oak door behind him and began to ascend to the clock. Touching the pistol wrapped in his pocket, the man moved to the door and slipped inside. It had never been locked from within, he knew. Far too much effort to turn the stiff and unwieldy key, his grandfather had told him during the Great War. Anyway what was there to steal? The rats? The staircase? Not a ten tonne timepiece, secure in its dusty, dark loft.

Softly the man climbed upwards. Above him he could hear the snuffling clockmaker, and could see the dim glow of the oil lamp he had lighted in the clock space.

He slipped his pistol from the leather cloth into his hand, a perfect weapon for his purpose, since it had no safety catch to give warning to those with keen ears. He stood silently at the top of the stairs.

Almost time.

As the great ratchet of the bell slipped on, the clockmaker sensed the presence behind him, and turned as the clapper fell, his mouth opened to scream. As the bell struck. Struck as loud as it had through wars and plagues, famine and pestilence, through sieges, rebellions, and the fall of Emperors.

Now it struck for death.

For one fate only.

One.

The first round ended the scream.

Two.

The second shot threw the clockmaker against the wall.

Three.

As the smashed body slumped to the floor, the man felt the recoil from the Parabellum round pull hard into his shoulder.

Four.

He fired again, synchronizing the last, as the first, with the deep crack of the great bell.

The brazen echoes faded slowly away.

Into stillness.

Silence.

The clockmaker trembled then moved no more.

Only the centuries counting, constant tick of the clock's engine disturbed the loft, above the barely audible moan of the night wind drifting across the rooftops. The man rewrapped the old, warm Polish gun in the soft leather, blew out the lamp and walked soundlessly down to the street door below.

He slipped outside and gently closed it behind him.

Pulling his greatcoat collar up around his neck, passing not one living soul, he walked away across the snow-quilted, hunched-back bridge over the ice-carapaced river, and into the maelstrom of the white winter's night.

Liberty

Llinos Jones

Finally you're free from these sullen hills,
Released from the burden of native pride.
Now purged of your roots, you've plunged into thrills
Unknown at home, with pleasure undenied.
New friends replace the old, new passions sought
With gait and voice, created and refined.
By measures close-studied and finely taught
You've shed your past with ease; you've found your kind.
But though your dreams may reach rich fulfilment
And through the years you'll steer this altered course
The caverns in your eyes voice the statement,
That none can claim a freedom from their source.
The fragile hooks of home remind your heart
That liberty's false joys shred souls apart.

My Doctor

Kay Barnes

My first Doctor was a repeated Jon Pertwee. I was six years old, too young to understand why this bizarre man with a full crop of fluffy white hair and the strangest clothes I had ever seen was running around in identical grey corridors. You hushed me gently, and enveloped my smaller shoulder in your hand until I settled back down from my curious bounce to watch the show. 'Watch it and find out,' you murmured patiently, and your wrinkled skin crinkled into whole new patterns as you pulled it back.

It was never long before I was fidgeting again, watching eagerly as the Doctor and his assistant ran away from the alien threat. Away from monsters that have only become plastic with an older, jaded eye. But back then I squealed with the assistant when some new threat bore down on her, and like thousands of others I dashed behind your armchair when the Daleks appeared, terrified that 'this' time the Doctor would lose and the Children of Davros would come for me. Before I got too big you would sometimes let me crawl onto your lap when the Daleks appeared, hushing Nan when she tutted about letting me watch something so frightening.

'Girls shouldn't be watching that sort of thing.' And she'd move to turn it off, only ever stopping when I dashed from hiding to sit still in the centre of the living room floor. I'd stay still until she left again with her blue teacup full, and then run back into hiding. It was more fun being scared, and you knew that. You always just smiled at me and let me play.

In the night it was Sea Devils I imagined coming after me, ready to drag me to a watery grave, and Bessie would come and rescue me from their clutches. You always chuckled gently when I told you about those nighttime imaginings, and asked all the right questions to change my nightmare into dreams of adventure the next night. I was a Time Lord in my dreams, thanks to you.

Until you got ill, we'd watch the different Doctors dance around the bad guys with just a sonic screwdriver and a bag of jelly babies each weekend, mugs of hot tea in front of us while Nan tutted away in the background.

These days I watch New Doctors dance with new steps. I watch them with new friends and coke instead of family and tea. But still when I hear that music start I can't help the eager bounce, and I can almost feel your hand on my shoulder again, calming me down to watch a brand new adventure. Someone beside me asks in a too-loud whisper, 'What's happening there?'

I smirk slightly behind my glass, thinking of you when I reply softly, 'Watch it and find out.'

Collect Call

Zara Little-Campbell

Your words creep over the Irish Sea –
Sluggish – they arrive as if by worn shoe;
Deep drawling sighs and panoramic
…Pauses
Punctuate coveted sentiments
Yet, the distance hollows the bond –
Quicker than the disembarking ferry.

Father

Zara Little-Campbell

He stole them from their beds
As clouds covered the night-sky,
He did it because he was a man
Losing sight, a man losing a life,
His great hurt countered with revenge;
A mother in the throes of mourning
For her brave little lost ones.

They took the ferry
To a world at war with England,
He was fleeing home,
And the children to a life of loss,
Where their small voices twisted
The knife in Ireland's dying fight.

The Taffia

Tyrone Deery

I was known by my chums as Typhoon Lagoon. Still to this day, I have no fucking idea what it meant. I led a gang of some of the school's most well-known characters. Pube and Gump were the muscle of my organization, lovely lads but neither playing with a full deck. If ever there was money needing to be collected, or if another scumbag from the school's long line of misfits took the liberty to bully one of our gang members, or more importantly, if they ever picked on one of our loyal customers, Pube and Gump would take it upon themselves to rough these idiots up. Not only were our customers buying quality products from our well-established company, they were also purchasing protection from these near to inbred, bullying misfits. Pube and Gump had perfected the fine art of 'wedgying'. I would have tears in my eyes, watching one of their victims scream, as his pants would be pulled so far up his back that it would finally come to rest on the top of his hapless head. Also in our gang was a small, odd-looking boy who we affectionately named Jaws. He was the finest gambler I had ever met, hence the name Jaws, a real shark. In all my school days, I never met a finer 'pitch and toss' player than he. He was a key asset to our gang, some weeks bringing in £40 plus from his gambling exploits. We had Lily, Lewy and Laskey who were the sales team. Fat Neil and Smelly Kelly who both helped us financially if we ever encountered any cash flow difficulties. (I would tell you how they came to gain all this spare money; however I would be putting both myself and them in some illicit difficulties, even after all these years. So mum's the word!) Young Spotted Dick Davies was another member. His name came about after a drunken shag with the school's most celebrated slag, Felicity Fist, who claimed Dick's dick was covered in puss-filled spots, which he has uncompromisingly denied to this day. He was a very clever boy, so I turned a blind eye to his spotted dick. I'd let him be in the gang as long as he kept his monstrosity far away from me. The final members of our gang were Big Al and Fat Allan. They were the comedy duo of the group, not an academic cell between them, but an unbelievable amount of wit and banter. Every gang needs a pair of clowns and we had the finest.

I remember the rival gangs in school, some of whom took themselves very seriously. These included 'The Panthers', 'The Daggers' and my personal favourite, 'The Taffia', fucking brilliant, you couldn't make this shit up. A lot of name calling and fist fights took place between our adversary gangs. Looking back and recalling how some of the names used to offend in these battles of wit still tickles me today. 'Gay Lord' has always stuck in my mind as being the harshest of this type of abuse, for not only are you homosexual, which was still frowned upon back then, but you are the lord of all homosexuals. You are the lord of the gays, the master, the god of all gays; you were being accused of having an overriding power that makes normal, decent people resort to this unearthly evil that is homosexuality. Of course as a silly, naïve child, not really understanding homosexuality, this is how your mind worked. Being ginger, I had my fair amount of abuse. From 'Carrot Head' to 'Ginger Minge' and 'Copper Knob' to 'Rusty Balls' the abuse was endless. Name calling was a massive part of school life and merit would be awarded for originality and bravery. Calling a teacher a name to his or her face was regarded as the ultimate gallantry. I remember being thrown out of an assembly and receiving a large spell of detention after shouting out to our new head of year, Mrs Avril Pickard, in the first assembly back after summer break, 'Avril Pickard makes my dick 'ard.' I know it's not big and I know it's not clever, but it was incredibly funny and very much worth it. The respect I gained from my peers after this one incident was incredible. This was the ultimate achievement. I was treated like a god.

I have nothing but fond memories of school. Even detention and suspension were, after the initial bollocking, fairly pleasant. I thrived in my school environment; this is where I truly came to life. Hated by my teachers, admired by my peers. I bought, sold and gambled. School for me wasn't so much about education; instead I concentrated much of my efforts on making money, being a nuisance and having an exceedingly smashing time. Money was my main aspiration in school. We loaned money to other kids (with our very own interest rate of course). We played cards and 'Pitch and Toss'. We would sell single cigarettes from anything between 50p and £2 a time.

We sold sweets, pop, crisps, dirty magazines, football cards and stickers, Top Trumps, Pogs, football shirts. You name it, we sold it. I bought and sold anything I could get my greedy little hands on; I was a right little 'Del Boy', a master at buying and selling crap. I could have sold onions to a man that doesn't even like onions but has had the misfortune to grow up on an onion farm and has been force fed onions for the past twenty-five years, because his onion-loving parents are too loyal to their beloved onion to give him anything but onion to eat.

Well that's enough shite about onions, what I'm trying to say is, I loved school. I loved everything about it. From the crap jokes to the mind-boggling lies told by some children. I had some boy trying to convince me that his dad had invented electric, what a dick! I even had some idiot trying to convince me that his family owned Wales and that they were thinking about selling it to the Queen, twat! Drugs in school was a funny subject, everybody thought they knew so much, when in fact no one had a fucking clue about anything. You would have young girls pretending they were off their tits after sniffing a 'Pritt-Stick'. Young lads smoking grass. Why's this funny, I hear you ask. Well this was no marijuana; this was indeed bog standard, rugby field grass, rolled up in a piece of A4 paper and then set alight. These idiots would lose both eyebrows, not to mention the damage they would do to their throats and the rugby field come to think of it. People pretending to be drunk was my personal favourite; these people had no shame. They would fall about, sing, dance, fight and pretend to cry after a can of Bass shandy, Muppets!

In all honesty Typhoon Lagoon himself did dabble in a small quantity of grass smoking and PVA sniffing. I must admit, I was just as fucking stupid as the rest of them. But who gives a fuck, that's what being in school is all about. I fucked off teachers, acted the twat, and went about my education generally being a childish cunt, but I fucking loved it. Where else in the world can you behave in this manner without getting into serious trouble? Nowhere! School was a breeding ground for little twats; we would fight, shag, swindle and steal. We got away with fucking murder, made a small fortune and had a fucking brilliant time doing it. School was fucking great!

Lucky Girl

Tommy Maguire

I went outside for a cigarette. The club was far too sticky with body heat for me, and the cool air outside became a pleasing counterpoint. It was so crisp that you couldn't really be sure when you'd stopped exhaling smoke and were just breathing out air.

Then I saw her, also smoking. Her cigarette just lit, barely a quarter gone when she dropped it to the ground and left it to smoulder. She was next to me immediately, asking me for a cigarette. I smiled, took one from my packet and lit it in her mouth. No words. She thanked me and walked off, glancing back once. I outed my fag and went back inside.

Twenty minutes later I saw her at the bar. I smiled again. 'Sinead,' she said. 'Stephan,' I looked at her, looked at the bar, looked at her, 'Shots?' She smiled.

We fucked. A couple of times. It wasn't the best, but it was a fuck. Filled a hole if you'll excuse the pun; the hole being Lisa. Lisa isn't here though. Lisa's gone. I just wanted a quick connection to someone; all I was craving was sex. Sinead knew this, could sense it, and that's why I'm alone in bed this morning. I phoned her a taxi late last night. I am, after all, a gentleman.

Lisa always stayed. I wanted her to. Wanted to feel her cheeks against my cock when I woke up. Then to wake her up kissing the top of her back, then small nibbles on her neck, snake my arms over and around so my fingers could dance between her breasts, sensitive places all. She'd roll over, groggy, and kiss my mouth as her hands went south to feel me ready, before climbing on top to wake us both up properly. These are the mornings I miss.

The last time someone who wasn't Lisa stayed was a fucking disaster. The girl was an absolute nut-job. Marissa. I'm not sure who picked up whom. I do know it was in the dingiest after-hours shit hole in town; drinking available 24 hours a day. Between midnight and six a.m. half pints of liquor only a fiver. For those on a mission to forget their own name it's the only place to be. I went there the night after Lisa left. I went home with Marissa. We were no sooner in the flat than she was stripping off, then straight onto her knees attempting to undo my belt buckle. I remember reality popping out for a minute at that point and peering down at the top of her head thinking 'Fucking hell, I've pulled a dwarf!' and also thinking that said 'dwarf' was attempting to fellate me from a standing position. It continued to go downhill from there. She wanted to insert things into me; these things ranged from her own digits to a carrot. I complied. It hurt. I fell asleep mid-shag and awoke at around eight a.m. to find myself alone and a carrot shoved halfway up my arse, thick end first. I yanked it out and went back to sleep. I awoke again a few hours later to feel someone riding me. I opened my eyes to see Marissa unwittingly recreating mine and Lisa's morning routine. It was different. I let her continue. We finished and she lay next to me. 'I'll come round tonight if you want?' Alarm bells rang, but not from the bedside table. 'Erm, no... I've got a girlfriend... sorry,' I mumbled feebly. She got out of bed, and if she had a hangover she wasn't showing it. She dressed quickly, and only stopped to hiss the word 'Prick' at me before leaving. I went back to sleep.

This morning however I am alone. The only traces of Sinead are a faint smell of perfume, two cigarettes in the ashtray with lipstick on them and three spunk-filled condoms on the floor. I open a window, empty the ashtray and dispose of the condoms. Sinead was never here.

It's just as well really. Sinead was a nice girl, but it could never have been anything other than a one-night stand. One lay. Well, three to be pedantic. Lisa gets back from holiday tonight, how could I explain another girl here in her bed? She's had ten days in Magaluf with the girls. I hope she enjoyed herself. She deserved that break, lucky girl.

Impenetrable Youth

Kay Barnes

Oh the young, and the beautiful,
The Old, and the dutiful,
They all come to you.
With your treasured hair, and your brooding flair
You're bored by anything new.

Like a moth to a flame, you're drawing me in
And you don't even know what you do.
It's so funny to me
That you don't know what you do.

Oh the young, and the beautiful,
The Old, and the dutiful,
They all come to you.
With your messed up hair, and your actor's flair
You haven't got a clue.

When you grin at me, your mask cracks and,
I'm Icarus too close to the sun.
You're so bad for me;
I wonder what I've begun.

Oh the young, and the beautiful,
The Old, and the dutiful,
They all come to you.
With your god damned hair, and your fucked up flair
You haven't got a clue.

Factory Time

David Emrys Davies

You haven't got a clue! Av ya boyo? You wanna know what work is ya little get? I'll tell you what work is. It's getting up every morning knowing that you're going to spend eight hours a day doing something you despise and the only thing that keeps you going is knowing that someday ya gonna get yourself out of that shit hole and do something with ya life. But what if that day never comes hey... ya fucked but. Don't get me wrong boyo, a man's allowed to dream. I had my own dreams when I was your age, I wanted to be a magician, but ya don't see me prancing about on stage pullin a rabbit from my arse do you son? Life doesn't work like that. You start work, earn a bit of money and just before you get something good sorted; ya misses knocks a couple of kids out. Then ya really up shit creek, you ain't even got an option. You have to work for bugger all until the bloody kids have grown up and fucked off. At this point you think, 'Wow, now I can really do something with my life.'... BULL SHIT! By the time the kids have gone you don't know how to do anything else. Ya too bloody old! It takes me an hour to get outta the fuckin chair!

But if ya think that's fuckin bad, let me tell you a story. There was this bloke right, worked in a factory for thirty-five years. He was about five foot two, bald head, scruffy, and had arms like two tree trunks. He kind of looked like penguin off batman, you'd think we would've called him penguin, but we just called him Cliff... anyway when he started, it was his job to hang big sheets of metal onto the moving hooks which would go into the paint plant to be sprayed. Cliff was awfully proud of what he did, but like any man you tend to get bloody sick of doing the same thing every day, especially when Cliff did the same thing for twenty years. If I was him I would have gone insane after the tenth year, but that's just me. So after his twentieth year of working at the factory the chairman had bestowed him with a gift to celebrate the time he'd served in the factory. And this gift was a beautiful gold watch.... A FUCKIN WATCH! No money, no trip to fuckin Magaluf, not even a couple of days off, a bloody watch. But they did give him the one thing he wanted, a different job, the one little thing in the world that would make his life that little bit more interesting. But they fucked it up! They put him on the other bloody side of the paint plant! Unhooking the bastard things! So don't come to me winging about ya job and braggin that ya gonna do something some day, cos it isn't gonna happen... idiot.

The River Suck

Zara Little-Campbell

Among the reeds he swims,
Naked, the cold clinging
To hairs on his back.
He submerges momentarily –
The gasp sounds out
As the ripples plunge to the surface;
His hair plastered over his face,
Arms stretched forward –
Almost in prayer, navigating
A path through murky waters.
Effortlessly he glides,
Disturbing nothing but silence;
This ritualistic nature retreat is
A Ballinasloe delicacy.
And the Suck takes its victims
Willingly – changing a person,
It replenishes hope; connects man
To the land and sea, a living
Body immersed in a beating world,
So cunning, we are blind to
Its timeless erosion.

The Road Rehearsed

Rob Morgan

Tom stood on the scruffy platform among the shuffling 'Sale'-destined crowds, as the empty train curved away along the winding track to the wet world's end.

No greeting.

No welcome.

No hope.

Shouldering his bag and his burden he walked into the shop-shuttered street past the lone 'strapper' leaning on his cab, and upwards towards a home long lost to him. Striding slowly where once he strutted, Tom stared, seeking a recognisable face, a glance of remembrance among the sullen shoppers shambling past pound shops, hairdressers and take-aways in the cold February rain.

None.

A long time.

Twenty years.

Resisting all attempts to revive hard memories, he glanced upwards at unfamiliar names on old shop fronts as he walked among and over the detritus of a small valley town's Saturday night.

Any number of Saturday nights.

Past desolate, fire-blackened 'Moriah' Tom tramped on. The 'Stute' stood silent, sealed and shell-shocked alongside it. But he couldn't shut out the sight of the place of his 'first', well, everything.

Girl.

Fight.

Pint.

And his last.

From here he left. Cheered on by less ambitious mates, and less-than-tidy girls, he sank the final bitter dregs of home, put his glass on the bar and walked to the Cardiff train.

She cried.

Twenty years ago.

Above him the long road led up Constitution Hill.

He stood and looked upwards, homewards, for the first time in all that time. Kicking an empty can into the streaming gutter he crossed the endless, eviscerated valley street and began to climb steadily towards 78, Cadwallader Terrace.

Slower now. Step by step. Slower.

A road remembered.

A road rehearsed.

A road untravelled.

Too late now, Tom.

The front door would be open he knew. They'd had to smash it in to get to her.

Too late.

Twenty years.

A visit too late.

He stooped for a moment resting against the wall by the boarded-up 'Bracchi' on the last corner before the house.

Tom lifted his head towards the wet fringe of the drizzling hill, where far up beyond his sight and reach a Council workman dug deep into the first turf of green grass, and the last.

For her.

He sobbed.

Just once mind.

Then drew a deep cold breath, shouldered his burden and walked onwards.

Skin

Enid Smith

Skin – a covering for the body – Everybody
    – every living thing.
Some thick and pachydermy, some soft and rather toady.
With hair it's said to be a pelt, with scales,
    a fish – or insect's wing.
There's wool for sheep – while feathers soft
    enable bird flight up aloft.

Some skins have prickles – some have slime
    – some, like flowers, are divine.
Trees have bark – their outer skin
    – the living skin is just within.

Our human races all have skin,
    sometimes it's thick, sometimes it's thin.
It may be black, or so-called white,
    which really truly isn't right,
For white is often tinged with red
    and even bears a yellow hue,
While black is really darkly brown,
    or coffee, cream or even tan
But often serves to do men down.

4,000 years back, men came from Africa's
        central plain to claim
New homes, new foods and ways of life
        saw always internecine strife,
With men who wanted more and more and crossed
        from land and shore to shore –
Today researchers now can trace our antecedents
        from that place.
We might be black or brown or white,
        beneath our skin we are alike,
But still we fight and slay, what shame,
        with knowledge broadened date by date,
It's time we learned to conquer hate.

It Was a Bargain, Love

Jo Perkins

'It must be the next turning,' Colin said, his patience beginning to run out.

Jeannie peered at the directions she'd printed off the website that morning. The route had seemed straightforward then, but now in the brief snatches of light from the street lamps, the neat lines and blocks bore no relation to the wet dark town surrounding them.

The streets were empty, of people and of any obvious landmarks. Even zealous bargain hunters had taken a look at the weather and decided to stay at home with the shopping channel instead. Some shopkeepers had decided to stop heating the street outside their premises and closed their doors, hoping that if no more desperate shoppers were blown into their premises, they might be able to sneak off home early for tea.

Jeannie looked affectionately at her husband, his face tired and cadaverous in the faint green glow from the dashboard lights. The trait of not throwing his money away on expensive sports cars that had seemed attractive when she first met Colin had become less appealing after five years of marriage. So his plans had come as a bit of a surprise.

'I'm taking you away for a special weekend. Splashing out on an expensive hotel. A Valentine's Day present, to show how much I love you.'

'But it's not Valentine's Day,' Jeannie replied, surprised and briefly overwhelmed by the sudden shower of money.

'It's much cheaper now, before the crowds. Valentine's Day gets booked up months in advance. We'll have a romantic break. A candlelit dinner, all the corny old stuff. Bracing walks on the beach.'

'Is it a luxury hotel?' Jeannie asked cautiously.

'Oh, it's the best. Loads of famous people have stayed there. Prime ministers, just everyone.'

Colin neglected to mention that this had been some years previously.

'It's even got a swimming pool. That's why I told you to bring your costume,' he added. 'You'll be able to have a dip if the weather's bad.'

Colin turned the car down a small alleyway by a sign pointing to the Crown Hotel car park. Of the hotel itself there was no evidence. They sploshed back to the street, bags in hand. Some hundred yards further down the street stood the Crown Hotel itself, faintly embarrassed that it now had to have a car park instead of stables for its guests' conveyances. Making the best of the circumstances, it tidied the cars neatly round the corner, out of sight into another century.

The spirits of the by-now somewhat damp and cold

travellers were cheered by the warm glow of lights spilling out of the large Georgian building. Inside, the tinsel that had clung desperately to the wall above the reception desk for several weeks was now beginning to admit defeat and swung lazily in the breeze from the open door. A Christmas tree stretched towards the ceiling dreaming of freedom. Knee deep in its own needles. It bent gently to one side, the result of some seasonal drunken embrace. It was, after all, nine days since Christmas.

'Nasty weather tonight, you'll be glad to be inside,' the receptionist chirruped. 'Your room's on the third floor, the lift's over there.'

'Thanks,' said Colin, looking at the battered metal lift doors, 'we'll walk.'

The stairs were wide enough to accommodate several hooped ball gowns at the same time, and Colin and Jeannie followed the slightly bare red turkey carpet for some miles. Up and around galleried landings and along corridors where they could have set up a golf driving range had they had the time to spare.

'I thought you'd want a room with a view, pet, I know how much you like the sea,' Colin said, as he fitted the key in the lock of the intricately colonnaded door.

Jeannie went towards the window and raised the substantial red and gold brocade curtain. She made a hole in the condensation on the window. The patch she had rubbed away was just enough for her to be able to see through to the condensation on the inside of the next pane of the double glazing. Releasing the catches on the window she poked a hand into the intemperate climate zone that existed between the two plates of glass and made another hole in the damp.

Beyond, black, nothing, no sea, just blackness. The Norse gods outside hissed and spat hard sleety rain at the window when they tired of banging loose drainpipes against the wall and kicking cans along the street.

'Don't you fancy a swim before dinner?'

Jeannie had noticed the pictures of the swimming pool which lurked in the basement, as attractive as a flooded dungeon.

'No I think I'll give it a miss. It's time to get changed for dinner.'

The waiter led them to a romantic and discreet table bang in the middle of the restaurant, next to a wooden parquet dance floor that had been buffed and battered by thousands of stilettos and dancing slippers over the years. The room was so huge that it could have comfortably hosted, at the same time, two wedding receptions of the more tacky kind, favoured by minor celebrity footballers. There would still have been room for a few coach loads of supporters. The white clothed tables marched into the distance, the neatly laid silver glinting in the light of the dusty candelabras. Jeannie wondered for a minute if it was a trick with mirrors. But it wasn't. The room was completely deserted.

She smiled at Colin and said, 'Darling, shall we dance before our prawn cocktail or after?'

They sat down, the waiter handed them a menu each and stood back for at least five seconds to let them consider their plight. As they looked at the slightly used menus, the doors opened and the room began to fill up slowly. Slowly, because the new arrivals had been claiming their pensions for many years.

The waiter leant over Jeannie's shoulder, 'I wouldn't have that if I were you,' he said, conspiratorially, pointing to the soup. Jeannie looked at him, hungry for more information on the exact nature of the problem. His face was expressionless. 'And the fish, it's off.' The waiter seemed pleased to have saved them a bit of time by reducing the choice.

'Oh we don't like eating our neighbours,' Colin said in a jovial fashion, gesturing towards the rattling shuttered seaward window.

Jeannie glanced over to the next table. An elderly woman sat eying her knife and fork suspiciously, her hair shining silver, her eyes milky blue. It did not seem entirely inconceivable that beneath her polyester pussycat bow there was a perfectly formed set of gills. And that, one starter, main course and sweet later, she would cast her crumpled serviette aside, leap up and with one flick of her fishy tail dive straight through the window into the wet night.

But the meal passed uneventfully and tastelessly. It moved at a pace not so sprightly that it would unsettle the regulars. The wait for their desserts was so long that Colin suspected the chef had nipped out to attend an evening class in something more interesting than catering.

But then the muffled muzak came to an abrupt halt and the quavering notes of an electric organ waltzed round the room.

'Tonight, we have on the drums, Mr Derek Davies! On electric guitar, the one and only Mike Jones! And tinkling the ivories, myself, Dougy Chapman!'

A light shone on the mature three-piece band in the corner. 'Oh my God!' cried Jeannie, sliding slowly down in her seat with embarrassment. 'You've brought me to a dinner dance!' Pair by creaking pair their fellow diners rose and made their way to the dance floor. Tight white curled heads bobbed, veined and wrinkled hands supported each other gently. The elderly couples smiled and swayed elegantly and expertly around the dance floor as they had done on each Friday evening for at least the previous half-century.

Jeannie relaxed as the realisation struck her that she would not have to dance and that their fellow diners were happy in a world of their own. They danced as they had since their youth with the occasional break to sit down and swap health notes.

'I told you I'd bring you somewhere special.' Colin emptied the remains of the bottle of house white into their glasses.

As they lay together in bed that night Jeannie turned to her husband. He lay on his back, mouth half open, snoring gently in a pig-like way. She smiled, rolled slowly out of the bed and pulled aside the heavy curtain. Outside snowflakes fell hesitantly and unhurriedly, partially obscuring the distant gleam of moonlight on the sea.

Drawing You (in Words)

Kay Barnes

I can't write a love story,
I've never been in love.

I can't write a fantasy,
All my fantasies are dead.

I can't write with passion,
My passion's all gone cold.

But still,
Ink falls from my pen.

Garbally Grounds

Zara Little-Campbell

So often have I, in ecstatic haste,
Taken leave of the present,
Transcendental flights, cryptic
Wanderings down beaten paths,
Always resting at the forty-two steps.
Walkways filled with seasonal joys,
A timeless picture that ages with
Muddied regret:

A place of beauty regimentally viewed
By stoic, cataract eyes. The weeping
Fields, imposing pillars, crude carvings in
The cobbled yard, impossible impending
Sights – the grand and miniscule.

Circling around the algae fish pond,

The slow trickling sprinkler becomes
A symbol to the days spent here.
The manor – an overshadowing
Conscience, a dark consideration
That on rare moments the top shutters
Crack open, revealing a titillating promise
– An interior so exotically intense.

And all the while St Joseph keeps
A faithful watch on the grassy slope,
Carved by hands made holy in the
Pursuit. The belt tight about the
Waist, more current of this Ireland,
As rain eats away glazed surfaces,
Eroding features and families.

After, and Afters

Alan Wakely

He lived for some years after he retired in the bungalow he bought with cash. He did not believe in borrowing. He did not subscribe to having now and paying later.

He would not entertain insurances, cars or televisions, and resented the impersonal machines that usurped men and horses in the winning of coal.

As the twentieth century crawled into view he was working in Lower Deep, a coalmine in Blaina, on the north-eastern edge of the South Wales coalfield. At thirteen years of age he was listed in the 1901 Census as 'a hewer of coal'.

Born of illiterate parents, history had a ready path carved for him and so many others.

You fell from a mother's womb and snatched your first screaming breath of coal dust, blessed to have lungs that knew they were alive.

If you survived your early months, if the rags that wrapped you did not become your winding sheet, you might live long enough to walk; if rickets did not enfeeble your bones leaving them too weak to keep you upright. If your father could stay alive long enough, if he could keep his limbs and lungs full with blood, food might grace your table, but always a crumb short of enough.

You had no choice. Your parents had no choice. Choice was on the master's table and the shelves in his pantry.

His children were conceived in the soft, indulgent folds of a feather bed, warmed by hot coals in a copper pan and fevered by a desire sanctified in the cold cavern of a church.

You were seeded when your mother spread her legs in the heather, frowned on by a God who neglected the charity of justice. For her, it was the sin of lust, for the wife of the master, it was a rightful purity. The wives of masters were forever virginal, chaste despite their writhings, safe in the hymned hypocrisy that made you a bastard.

But, somehow, when the words came to your eye, when numbers no longer spoke from your fingers, when you could piss like a man, after these, you found another way.

In 1954 you retired to that bungalow. You had earned your way from coal hewing boy to manager, qualifying as a mining engineer on the way and becoming the youngest qualified mine manager in the South Wales coalfield. It was a remarkable journey that took you to that bungalow with its bay windows, lawns, prim and primrose'd borders, gooseberries, blackcurrants and a fat-fruited strawberry patch.

High on the hill it had air and light and Sunday tea. The

family would arrive and sit at oak, the table a testimony to harvests, beetroot and tomato juiced, layered with cooked ham and mature Cheddar from the Home and Colonial that made my gums itch. You bought the best. You shopped at the best. You grew the best.

But for 'afters'. Why tinned apricots? And Carnation tinned milk?

Over-sweet, syrupy, not the sharp and clean strawberries from your own garden with the home-made cream she used to make.

I remember a sweet shudder, from hair-root to toe, when biting into those scarlet globes sneaked out of sight of a scolding. The smell of mint, sage and thyme light on an evening breeze. Wind-whipped sheets with the bouquet of a summer sun; and the steam whistles when she walked me past the mine to the shops a mile away, the men driving the engines saluting her majesty as she passed, doffing their caps.

And the kitchen, floured and misted, one-eyed jars of homemade everything sitting on shelves, guardians of culinary probity. The nights when put to bed, the air full with the sounds of crickets' arias interwoven with the rhapsody of rustling leaves; and a kiss, a love token on my pillow promising a new day with toast made from locally baked bread – scorched on coals as fierce as lava – that leaked salty butter onto a cooling plate.

So, why? From tins? Is this what happens when one ceases work and goes to live in a bungalow?

My memories are not for tins, they are not from tins, they cannot be tinned...

At the bottom of the garden, half-submerged in the hedge was the shed. Inside he kept his tools, shears as sharp as frost, a lawn mower that whisked and whirred as it cut; guillotined grass brave enough to grow more than an inch. Saws. Wooden handled forks. Some small, some large. Each had its purpose, specific to the task, clean bladed, lightly oiled and hung on nails of equal length. It was order, not tidy, it was more.

He won prizes with that garden and its produce, never first prize, always second or third, and resolutely, the strawberries remained cream-free.

She used to sneak them. She would waddle – she had aged – down the path to hang something wet and dripping on the line. She would drop a peg, tut-tut fit for an Oscar, then root around the strawberries, some ten feet away, for the recalcitrant peg, rising triumphant and wiping her lips, waving the peg, shouting for God himself to hear: 'There we are then, I've found it, don't worry!'

I do not think he was amused, annoyed or moved to despair over such a poor performance, it happened and that was that. Come the end of the season, she would have to go without. The rest of us would not notice the loss, and other than the arrival of the first fall of snow that turned the world to pastry, the season ebbed away on the autumn burnished flanks of the hill.

In the spring of 1963 he died. It is odd to recollect the decline in the place. The garden decayed and the shed slowly eased itself deeper into the hedge and took with it his once pristine tools and his care.

My grandmother bought a television and took religion with Songs of Praise; and a more secular delight in the crotch of Nureyev when ballet flickered on screen. The old black-leaded cooking range was ripped out and replaced with a tiled monstrosity that had much in common with a public lavatory, with not a trace of marmalade to traitor my attempts at cooking tarts.

The lawns were cut, but no borders edged or bushes pruned. My father would call once a week and I would see the sadness in his face, and the guilt. And he need not have felt that way, it was unfortunate but, no longer was there time for strawberries, they had anyway, run wild and ragged, not fit to produce fruit. A strawberry became a rare thing to see, and scarce to the tongue.

But we did have strawberries and cream at the funeral... out of tins.

Grandma Catteral

Enid Smith

Long black coat, black boots, black hat.
Pale face, long and slightly square.
Deep lines in cheeks and on her brow,
Her lips are modelled, wide her mouth
But Ugh! her sloppy kisses!

No rings but wedding
Up-piled hair – hands strong and firm and mannish.
Quite tall, her body strong, erect;
Determined, forceful gains respect.

Strong on chapel, Sankey's hymns;
Wicked children, inborn sins.
Look with eyes and not with fingers.
Don't answer back, do as you're told;
Children should be seen not bold.

You say you've tried, you've done it right
But that's no good – it could be better
Just tear it up and try again
And say your prayers... Amen... Amen.

Snapshots

Laura Thompson

Freedom

I counted down the days until I could leave home. I packed all the stuff I needed and gave away the rest. I rolled up all my yellowed posters of the places I would visit and placed them safely in a cardboard holder that I slid into my only suitcase. My family and boyfriend drove me to the airport. They all had tears dripping from their cheeks and noses, but my eyes remained as dry as a good red wine. We hugged for a final time, and then it was time to board. They had to push me through the gate.

Honesty

My best friend gave me back her half of the best friend heart necklace. She said she had a new best friend now and it wouldn't be right for her to keep it. I put the two broken heart halves into a box and closed the lid. When I saw her ten years later working at the local grocery store, I smiled and bragged a little more than needed about my success. At home, I opened the lid of the box that had been closed for ten years, and then shut it again. What do you do with two broken hearts?

Cover Up

When I woke up in the morning, I never liked what I saw. So I immediately put my pretty face on. I laid the foundation for a better me and built shields with mascara, powder, and concealer. Eyeliner and blush boosted my confidence better than a Long Island Iced Tea. With my pretty face on, I could face co-workers, friends, my mailman, or my television screen. When I felt my mask cracking, I repaired it instantly, constantly dreading the day's end, when my pretty face would be washed down the drain. In the meantime though, I smiled with stained pink lips.

Memories

When my grandfather got old, he got mean. He got deaf and forgetful and frank. We used to visit every Sunday and stay all day, but near the end, he would tell us to leave when he got tired. He used to make us tea and cookies, but near the end, my dad had to do that part. When I talk about my grandfather now, I tell stories about the man who played with us all day long, the man who made me special snacks, the man whom I endlessly admired. I rewrite the story and end it before the end.

The Pictures Not Taken

Zara Little-Campbell

If Frost can do it then so can I,
Contemplate the road until I die:

If I had taken the pictures that I had not
I'm sure life's details would not be forgot.

They would be the hidden locket
The uncovering of receipts found in the pocket;

They would show your reproachful glare
Perhaps even allude to your bursts of care.

They would scream of quality bonding
Loc-Tite; a family no longer responding;

They would freeze-frame your body's tension
As your son's face grew beyond mention.

They would be the poster of your fears
The stagnant expression of lingering peers,

They would crystallise the clink of cups
Depicting the years when you had enough.

They would sing of picnics in Coole Park
How we lost the car as it suddenly grew dark;

They would show how the seasons bled –
How hope discoloured to resemble lead.

They would encapsulate the immense
moment of your short laughter.

How your hair dramatically greyed
And at the seams life enviably frayed...

These should be the album of conscience –
Wise mind scrambled them to little more than nonsense.

Contributors

Kay Barnes has been a bookworm since youth, but it was only in 1999 that she discovered a passion for creating and writing her own stories. She loves the exhilaration of challenging someone who really knows what they're doing, and takes this into all aspects of her life; especially writing, activism and medieval sword fighting. Kay loves to sing but at the insistence of friends and family only does so when alone, or drunk.

David Emrys Davies graduated from Trinity College, Carmarthen with a B.A. (Hons) Degree in Theatre Studies. During this course, he put on several productions, including *The Long and the Short and the Tall* by Willis Hall and *Animal Farm* by George Orwell. David also helped devise a TIE touring production called *This is the Army Mr. Jones*, which was based on Conscription during the 1950s. David now hopes to become a playwright and continue his acting after his Masters in Creative Writing.

Tyrone Deery was born and bred in the little springshine town of Merthyr Tydfil and discovered this quite unique talent of being able to read and write. The masses cried, 'Son, don't waste this gift, go share your knowledge, however – please take it easy on the word cunt, we've got a bad enough reputation as it is.' Tyrone wanders lonely in a bra, but he's beginning to suspect that his solitude is a direct result of his unhealthy bra addiction.

Katy Griffiths was born and brought up in Pembroke Dock. She graduated from Trinity College, Carmarthen in 2007 with a B.A. in English and Creative Writing, where she discovered that she could add plays, short stories and a novella to her writing repertoire. She draws inspiration from everything and everyone around her; therefore, family and friends could recognise themselves in her writing. Whether they take that as a compliment or not is up to them!

Llinos Jones has spent umpteen years as an English teacher encouraging others to write and explore their creative skills. She decided last year that her writing needed to see daylight, enrolled on the MA Creative Writing course and is now frantically trying to craft some decent poetry (and some prose in passing).

Zara Little-Campbell is a poet and fiction writer from Co. Galway in Ireland. The last four years of her life have been dedicated to pursuing the disposition of the Irish writer. She feels she has mastered some aspects more so than others, but refuses to divulge the particulars. She has completed her BA in Creative Writing and English in Trinity College, Carmarthen and is currently undertaking the MA Creative Writing programme.

Tommy Maguire was born in the mid 80s in London to Irish parents. He proceeded to dislike school in its academic sense, and failed most of his GCSEs. He managed to blag his way into doing four A levels. This quickly became three. After a lot of luck, he moved to Carmarthen, Wales to study Theatre. Four years later, he's somehow a writer. Now 22, he's still in Carmarthen studying for his Masters in Creative Writing.

Rob Morgan, after careers in teaching, youth and community work and politics, is now Director of the 'Wales! Look East!' Project, working in Western Ukraine. A life-long bibliomaniac, he describes his interests as medieval music, naval history and game playing. Rob's ambitions, should he ever be asked, are to become a 1st Kyu level player of the ancient Japanese game *GO*, to own a hot-air balloon and to be able to explain the offside rule in Association Football.

Jo Perkins was born in Scunthorpe, Lincolnshire. Following an English degree at University College, Swansea, she decided to avoid the world of grown-up work and became a journalist instead. The years she spent producing television news reports with BBC correspondents then made life with a houseful of toddlers a peaceful and strangely attractive option. She now lives very close to the sea in West Wales with her husband, three children and assorted cats.

Jan Slade loves to write, and a childhood in Africa, a peripatetic lifestyle and a weird and wonderful career path have all combined to give her a wealth of experiences to draw on. After moving to Wales eight years ago, she is now settled and at last able to fulfil her ambition of attending university, yet another experience to add to her cache.

Enid Smith graduated from the University of Bristol in 1976 with a degree in Environmental Science. She has since turned to writing and has had several poems and short articles published in anthologies and magazines. In addition to writing, she loves the countryside, reading, horses, dogs, music and painting.

Penny Sutton comes from a long career in numbers, followed by a shorter career in garden design. Now in semi retirement, she enjoys manipulating the written word, inspired by several decades of living as an expatriate in sub Saharan Africa, as an itinerant in England and, more recently, as an incomer to Wales.

Laura Thompson is a Canadian writer looking for inspiration in Wales. She earned an Honours BA in English Rhetoric and Professional Writing with a minor in French from the University of Waterloo (Canada) and has worked as a government researcher, English tutor, marketing writer and even an ice cream server in France. She is currently enjoying a quieter life writing creatively for the MA programme, spending time with her fiancé and spending energy raising her beautiful puppy.

Alan Wakely was born in 1948 and will be older this year than last, but with few distinguishing marks. He has done many different things, and the Revenue are still trying to prove it. He has always had some notion that writing was important to him, but only during the last three years has he done something positive about it. He has a 1930s car that has him enraptured about rust, woodworm and disintegrating organic material. He does not send Valentine cards or flowers, and an ingrowing toenail still troubles him.

Acknowledgements

The editors and contributors would like to extend their gratitude to Trinity College, Carmarthen for its support of this anthology, and in particular M.A. Creative Writing Course Directors Menna Elfyn and Dr Paul Wright for their guidance and encouragement throughout this project and Kevin Matherick, Head of Faculty of Arts and Social Sciences, for his support. We would also like to thank Dominic Williams and Lucy Llewellyn at Parthian for their invaluable contribution and their repository of expertise, essential in the production of *Rewind*.

We would like to show our appreciation for all those others who offered support and assistance in the production and promotion of this anthology.

Finally, to the *Rewind* committee – Laura Thompson, Zara Little-Campbell, Kay Barnes, David Davies, Tyrone Deery, Tommy Maguire, Rob Morgan, and Alan Wakely – a special thanks for your commitment and enthusiasm.

Second thoughts are best. – Lord Byron